A Splash of Forever

To Pixie and Fonzie—crazy tabby clowns.

GROSSET & DUNLAP
Published by the Penguin Group
Penguin Group (USA) LLC, 375 Hudson Street, New York, New York 10014, USA

USA | Canada | UK | Ireland | Australia | New Zealand | India | South Africa | China

penguin.com
A Penguin Random House Company

Text copyright © 2008, 2014 Sue Bentley. Illustrations copyright © 2008 Angela Swan. Cover illustration copyright © 2008 Andrew Farley. All rights reserved. First printed in Great Britain in 2008 by Penguin Books Ltd. First published in the United States in 2014 by Grosset & Dunlap, a division of Penguin Young Readers Group, 345 Hudson Street, New York, New York 10014. GROSSET & DUNLAP is a trademark of Penguin Group (USA) LLC. Printed in the USA.

Library of Congress Cataloging-in-Publication Data is available.

ISBN 978-0-448-46797-9   10 9 8 7 6 5 4 3

A Splash of Forever

SUE BENTLEY

Illustrated by Angela Swan

Grosset & Dunlap
An Imprint of Penguin Group (USA) LLC

As a terrifying roar sounded, there was a bright flash and a dazzling shower of sparks. Where the young white lion had been, there now stood a tiny, fluffy gray-and-white kitten with bright emerald eyes.

Flame trembled, hoping that his kitten disguise would protect him from his uncle. Keeping his belly low to the ground, he crept into the entrance of a nearby cave and hid behind a large rock.

Outside Flame could hear heavy
paws thudding over the stony ground. A
dark shadow with a thick mane appeared
at the mouth of the cave.

"Ebony!" Flame gasped, pressing
his tiny body more tightly against the
sheltering rock.

The adult lion sniffed the air and
gave a low growl as it entered the cave.
Flame stiffened. This was it! He was
going to be found and dragged outside.

Suddenly a huge paw, as big as Flame
was now, reached around the rock and
scooped out the kitten.

"Prince Flame, I am glad to see you
again, but it is not safe for you to be
here," the adult lion rumbled.

"Cirrus!" Flame mewed with relief.
"I thought my uncle had found me!"

Cirrus's gray muzzle crinkled in a fond smile as he encircled the kitten with his powerful paws. "While I live I will protect you, but Ebony will never stop looking for you. He wants to keep ruling in your place."

Flame's emerald eyes flashed with anger. "Perhaps it is time for me to face him and take back the Lion Throne!"

"Bravely said," Cirrus growled softly, his tired eyes narrowing with pride. "Use this disguise and go back to hide in the other world. Return when you are strong and wise and *then* save the land from your uncle's evil rule."

Before Flame could reply, a thunderous roar split the air. There came the sound of mighty paws on rock, and the ground shook as a heavy animal jumped to the ground outside the cave.

"Ebony is very close. Go, Flame. Save yourself!" Cirrus urged.

Bright silver sparks ignited in the tiny, fluffy gray-and-white kitten's fur. Flame whined softly as he felt the power building inside him. He felt himself falling. Falling . . .

Chapter
ONE

As Alice Forester listened to her teacher, she felt her heart sinking.

"Now that the new pool's ready for use, we'll be starting swimming lessons tomorrow. So don't forget your bathing suits!" Ms. Ritson said. She had a bright, smiling face and very straight brown hair that she wore tied back.

"Oh, that's just what I need—not!"

Alice grumbled. She had only just moved to this school and had been really pleased to find that she wasn't going to be having swimming lessons.

Her tummy had gone all squirmy at the thought of the pool of blue chlorine-scented water. *It's all right for the other kids*, she thought. *No one's going bully* them *for being better than everyone else at swimming.*

"Yay! I can't wait to get in the new pool. We can do mega cannonballs and have shoulder-stand fights in the shallow end!" shouted Tim Wagnall.

"Now, Tim. You know very well that kind of dangerous behavior isn't allowed," Ms. Ritson said, giving him one of her looks.

"Too bad!" Tim said cheerfully.

Everyone laughed, and even Alice found herself grinning. Tim was always messing around and playing tricks. He could be annoying sometimes, but he was really funny.

"And I've got even more exciting news," Ms. Ritson went on. "We're having a grand reopening ceremony for the new pool, and as part of

that there's going to be a swim meet.
Everyone's going to take part!" She
smiled brightly at the class. "I can see
a few of you looking a bit concerned,
but don't worry. There's a new after-
school swimming club on Mondays,
Wednesdays, and Fridays. I'll be coaching,
and I'd like you all to try to come to
a couple of sessions."

Some of the kids cheered. Tim
stood up and ran around wind-milling
his arms as if he was doing freestyle
swimming, which made everyone laugh
again.

Everyone except for Alice. She felt
as if her grin had frozen on her face. This
was her worst nightmare coming true.

Ms. Ritson clapped her hands for
silence. "Calm down, everyone. I'd like

you to take out your books and start work please." As the class settled down, she came over to Alice's desk. "Are you feeling okay, Alice? I noticed that you looked a little anxious when I was making the announcements."

"I'm not, ma'am," Alice said. "It's because . . . I'm . . . um, not allowed to go swimming. I've got this . . . um, really thin blood. It's awful. The minute I get in the water my legs go all white and shaky, like cooked spaghetti, and my lips go blue and swell up like great big slimy slugs."

Ms. Ritson frowned. "That sounds alarming. I assume we have a doctor's letter about that or a note from your mom, excusing you from swimming? I'll check the school records."

Alice gulped. "I haven't exactly been to the doctor. And Mom did write a note, but I lost it when . . . um, a dog grabbed it and ran away with it on the way to school."

"Is that right?" Ms. Ritson said, looking skeptical.

"Yes," Alice carried on desperately. "And I probably can't come to after-school club, either. I have to pick up my brother after school and keep an eye on him. Mom's a single parent and she babysits Esme and Luke during the week, so . . ."

Ms. Ritson smiled patiently. "I'm fully aware of your home situation, Alice. Swimming club will be open until eight tonight. I'm certain that if you explain to your mom how important this is, she'll

make sure you can fit in an hour's practice
here and there."

"Yes, ma'am," Alice mumbled glumly
as the teacher moved away.

She sighed, wishing that her best
friend from her old school, Holly, was
still here. She would understand.

Alice felt her eyes prick with tears,
but swallowed hard and began outlining
a swirling Celtic design in black marker.

Tim Wagnall sauntered past her
desk. Reaching back with one hand, he
flipped Alice's workbook onto the floor.

"Oh!" Alice's black marker had
skidded across the diagram, ruining all
her careful work. "You idiot! I'll have
to do it all again now!" she said angrily.

"Tough!" Tim snickered.

As Alice bent down to pick up the
book, Tim kicked it farther under her
desk. Alice had to get down on her
hands and knees to reach for it.

Tim was still standing there with
a silly grin on his face when she
sat down again. "Buzz off," she said
irritably.

Tim rolled his eyes before walking
away. "Huh! Some people can't take
a joke."

"Yeah? Well, you're about as funny
as catching the plague!" Alice muttered
under her breath.

A minute later, a rubber band pinged
Alice's arm. When she looked over at
Tim, he was innocently looking out the
window.

When the bell rang at the end of
school, Alice headed for the path that led

to her brother Ben's classroom. The school's garden filled the square space between the two school buildings. Still worrying about the swim meet, Alice wandered through the peaceful garden past some rows of tall green beans.

Just as she reached a bench in the garden, there was a bright flash and a big spurt of silver sparks.

"Oh!" Alice blinked, blinded for a moment.

She looked over her shoulder to see if Tim Wagnall was lurking nearby—it would be just like him to follow her and set off a firecracker as a prank. But there was no one else around.

When Alice turned back to the bench, she saw a tiny kitten with gray-and-white fur, a cute pink nose, and emerald eyes. Hundreds of tiny sparkles, like miniature fireflies, gleamed in its fluffy coat.

Alice frowned. She was sure that she hadn't seen a kitten there a minute ago.

"Where did you just come from?" she murmured wonderingly.

The kitten stood up and arched its tiny back. "I have come from far away. Can you help me?" it mewed.

Chapter
TWO

Alice stared down at the kitten in surprise. She must be hearing things. She was sure there was no one else in the garden who could be playing a prank on her.

Alice reached for the kitten to pick it up. *It's just a normal kitten—probably a stray,* she told herself. Its gray-and-white fur was warm, and it was as soft as

goose down. She felt a tiny, fast
heartbeat ticking against her fingers.

"Please, can you help me?"

Alice's eyes widened with shock at
the little voice. She put down the kitten
hastily but gently and took a step back.
"H-how c-come you can talk?" she
stammered.

The kitten pricked its tiny ears. "In
my world all the big cats can talk. My
name is Prince Flame. What is yours?"
it mewed again.

Alice gulped. Talking cats did not
just appear to ordinary schoolgirls in
gardens! But this kitten had, and it was
blinking up at her expectantly, waiting
for her answer.

"I'm A-Alice Forester," she found
herself replying.

"Alice, I am honored to meet you,"
the kitten purred. "Where is this place?"
Despite Flame's tiny size, Alice thought
that he seemed strangely unafraid of her.

"Meldway School. In Northampton,"
she replied. "That's my classroom behind
us." She felt confused. "Did . . . did you
just say that you're *Prince* Flame?"

The kitten lifted its head and its bright
emerald eyes gleamed with pride. "Yes.
I am heir to the Lion Throne. But my

uncle Ebony has stolen it from me and
rules in my place."

Alice was still having trouble taking
everything in. "No offense, but you seem a
bit small to be the ruler of anywhere," she
said.

Flame drew himself up indignantly.
"Stand back, please."

As Alice stepped backward, Flame
jumped down from the bench. There was
another bright flash and a big whoosh
of silver sparks that crackled as they hit
the grass.

"Oh!" Alice was blinded for a moment.

When her sight cleared, she saw that
in the tiny kitten's place stood a regal
young white lion. Its thick velvety coat
looked as if it had been sewn from
thousands of twinkling stars. Then just

as suddenly as the majestic lion had
appeared, Flame returned as the fluffy
gray-and-white kitten with a cute
pink nose.

"Flame? Was that you?" Alice gasped.
"You really are a lion prince!"

Flame nodded, and she could see
that his tiny kitten body was starting to
tremble. "I am in danger from my uncle's
spies. If they find me, they will kill me.
Will you keep me safe?"

Alice felt her heart go out to him. As
a young white lion, Flame was awesome.
Disguised as this cute fluffy kitten, he
was adorable. "Oh, of course I will. You
can come and live with me."

More confidently this time, she
picked him up and gently stroked the
top of his head. Flame began purring

and rubbing his head against her arm.

"Hey! I thought you were supposed to be picking me up!" called an annoyed voice.

Alice looked around to see a six-year-old blond boy running toward her. It was Ben. Her brother got his blue eyes and floppy fair hair from their mom. Their dad had had brown eyes and springy dark hair; Alice took after him.

"What are you doing over here?" Ben asked. Then he saw Flame. "Cool! Where did you get that kitten?"

"I was on my way over to meet you when I found him. He's called Flame. And he can ta—" Alice began, but suddenly Flame reached up and tapped her cheek with one tiny front paw.

"Meow-ow-ow!" he said loudly,

looking up at her with pleading emerald eyes and shaking his head.

Alice looked down at Flame, confused, before suddenly realizing that he didn't want her to tell Ben about him. She patted him reassuringly, letting him know that she understood.

Ben looked at Flame with puzzled blue eyes. "Why's it making that noise?

Can I stroke it? Are we going to take it home?"

"*Him*, not *it*. And he's got a name," Alice corrected. "Yes, we're taking Flame home. He can live in my bedroom," she said, but then she remembered their mom's strict rules about not having pets. "Listen to me, Ben," she said, kneeling down to look him in the eyes. "This is really important: We're not going to tell Mom about Flame, okay?"

"Great. Flame's really cute, isn't he? We can share him," Ben said, not really paying attention.

"Ben! If Mom finds out about Flame, she'll make us take him to the animal shelter. Do you understand that?" Alice said seriously.

"Of course I do!" Ben said. "I won't tell *anyone* about him. Cross my heart and hope to die!"

"Okay then. And you have to do what I tell you to with Flame. No grabbing him and taking him out to play in the garden or dashing around to your friend's house with him, without asking me first."

"I don't see why you're in charge!" Ben said, sticking out his bottom lip.

"It's because I found Flame, and anyway, I'm older than you," Alice said. "Deal?"

Ben kicked at some grass with the toe of his sneaker. He nodded. "Deal."

Alice gave a relieved sigh. "Right. Let's go home." She opened her shoulder bag, so Flame could jump inside. "There

you are. Nice and safe," she whispered
as he settled in. As she and Ben started
for home, Alice put her hand inside her
bag and stroked Flame. He was curled up
beside her pink velvet pencil case. She
smiled as she felt him purring contentedly,
but she wished that Ben didn't know
about him.

There was nothing she could do
about it now. She really hoped that Ben
would remember his promise not to
tell anyone about Flame—especially
their mom.

"Hi, Mom—we're home!" Alice
called as she and Ben came into the house.

"Hi, Mom. Later!" shouted Ben,
clomping straight up the stairs.

"Hello, you two!" Mrs. Forester's

voice floated out of the kitchen.

Alice popped her head around the door. Her mom was cooking supper. Esme and Luke sat in their high chairs, picking at little piles of carrot, apple, and grated cheese.

"How are the terrible twins?" Alice said, bending down to give them each a kiss on the cheek. "Have you been good for my mom today? Have you?"

The twins gave her gummy grins. Esme held up a tiny bit of carrot between her finger and thumb. "Ally want?"

"Mmm. Yum, yum. Delicious," Alice said, nibbling at the chubby fingers and pretending to eat.

As Esme squealed with delight, Mrs. Forester smiled and tucked a strand of her curly fair hair behind her ears.

"It feels like it's been a long day," she said with a sigh. "How was school?"

"Okay. Nothing special," Alice said vaguely, deciding not to mention anything about the dreaded swimming lessons, the after-school swimming club, or the meet. Somehow all that seemed a lot less important than finding Flame.

"I'm just going upstairs to get changed, Mom. I'll only be a minute," she said as she went into the hall. She looked inside her bag as she went upstairs. "I'll make you a cozy bed on my comforter, Flame."

"Thank you, Alice," Flame mewed softly. "I am feeling tired after my long journey."

Ben followed Alice into her bedroom. "Get Flame out. I want to play with

him," he cried eagerly.

"*Shhh!* Mom will hear you," Alice
whispered. "Not now. Let Flame settle
in first. He said that he's . . . I mean,
he's probably tired," she corrected herself
hastily. "Kittens need lots of sleep,
you know."

"But I want to play with him now,"
Ben protested.

"Well, you can't. Maybe later," Alice said firmly.

"He's my kitten, too. Not just yours!" Ben snapped.

Alice made herself answer calmly. "Of course he is. Why don't you come with me to buy Flame some food later?"

Ben brightened. "Okay then. Can I choose what kind to get him?"

Alice nodded.

Ben went toward the door. "I'm going to ask Mom if I can go to Dean's house to play now."

"Don't say a word to him about Flame," Alice cautioned. "Dean's mom talks to our mom."

"I'm not stupid!" Ben scoffed, leaving her room.

Alice heard him go into the

bathroom and close the door. A minute later, the toilet flushed and she heard the faucet being turned on. Then Ben came out and went downstairs.

Alice sat on her bed beside Flame, who was fluffing the comforter with his tiny gray-and-white front paws. "Ben's already being a pain about you living here. But at least he thinks you're just a normal kitten."

Flame nodded. "It is good that you did not tell Ben about me. You must never tell anyone my secret. Promise me, Alice."

Alice nodded. "No one's ever going to hear about you from me, I promise. You're safe with me."

"Thank you, Alice. I think I'll take a nap now." Flame gave her a whiskery grin and tucked his nose into his paws before settling down to sleep.

As Alice looked at him, a bubble of happiness rose up from inside her. In her wildest dreams, she had never imagined that her new best friend would be a magic kitten!

Chapter
THREE

Leaving Flame on her bed, Alice quickly changed into jeans and a T-shirt and went downstairs.

In the kitchen, her mom was giving Esme and Luke some drinks in plastic cups.

Alice filled the kettle at the sink. "I'll make us some tea."

Her mom smiled. "Great! I could

really do with one. The twins' mom just called to say she's stuck in traffic on the highway, so she could be an hour late. I said Esme and Luke could have supper with us."

Alice thought her mom looked tired. Ben was a handful, even without looking after two toddlers all day.

Alice checked the saucepan on the stove.
"I think these potatoes are done. Do you
want me to mash them?"

"Would you, honey? Thanks,"
Mrs. Forester said.

"No problem," Alice said. She liked
helping her mom. It made her feel grown-
up. After she'd made the tea and mashed
the potatoes, Alice started cleaning up.

"I think Luke's diaper needs
changing. I'll take him to the bedroom."
Mrs. Forester lifted the little boy out
of his chair.

Just then, Alice saw a big drop of
water plop onto the draining board. She
frowned as another drop splashed next to
it, and then another. Looking up at the
ceiling, she saw another drop squeezing
through a tiny hole. "Mom, look! Water's

dripping from somewhere!"

Mrs. Forester glanced up and cried out in dismay. "It's coming from the bathroom. Someone must have left the faucet running!"

"And I know who. Ben!" Alice was already half out of the kitchen and hurtling up the stairs.

As she reached the landing, she saw water pouring out from the open bathroom door.

"May I help?" Flame mewed from her bedroom doorway, looking bright-eyed and alert after his nap.

"Mom's right behind me! It's probably best if you just hide," she whispered.

Flame gave a determined purr and time seemed to stand still.

Alice watched in amazement as
huge bright silver sparks ignited in
Flame's gray-and-white fur; his whiskers
crackled with electricity. She felt a
warm prickling sensation down her
spine.

Something strange was going to
happen!

In what seemed like slow motion,
Flame leaped toward the bathroom,
trailing sparks like a silver comet. "Do
not worry," he called. "I will use my
magic to make myself invisible. Only
you will be able to see and hear me,
Alice!"

Alice went into the bathroom and
stood there in amazement.

Flame stood on the edge of the
bathtub, balancing on his back legs.

Silver sparks were shooting out of
his front paws and filling the entire
bathroom. They whirled around busily,
like millions of little bright worker bees.

Squeak! The faucet turned itself
off. *Shloop!* The water in the sink was
slurped down the drain. *Sploosh!* A big
silver cape of water droplets rose from
the carpet and swirled itself into the
bathtub, where it collapsed and drained
away.

"Wow! This is *so* amazing!" Alice
breathed.

Flame jumped down from the
bathtub and stood beside Alice. Just as
the last bright spark faded from his fur,
Mrs. Forester appeared at the top of the
stairs, carrying Luke.

She gaped at the spotless bathroom.

"So, where's that water in the kitchen coming from?"

"Condensation," Alice blurted out. "We did an experiment on it last semester."

She bit back a grin at the thought that Flame was sitting there large as life, but her mom obviously couldn't see him!

"I suppose it's possible," Mrs. Forester said, looking puzzled. "Oh well, I'm just glad we haven't got a full-scale flood on our hands. I'd better see to Luke. Could you go down and keep an eye on Esme for me please, honey?"

"Sure thing!" As Alice went downstairs, Flame scampered after her. As soon as they were alone, she picked him up and cuddled him. "Thanks, Flame. You were amazing!"

Flame rubbed his head against her hand. "You are welcome."

✦

The following morning Alice woke to the sound of loud purring close to her ear. Rubbing her eyes, she sat up and reached out to stroke Flame. "Did you sleep well?"

Flame stuck all four paws out and stretched his legs. "Yes, thank you. I feel safe here," he mewed.

"Good. Maybe your uncle's enemies will stop looking for you," Alice said, gently stroking his tiny ears. "Then you can stay here forever."

A troubled expression crossed Flame's tiny face. "Ebony's spies will not stop until they find me. But even if they didn't find me, I could not stay. I must return to my own world one day and take back my throne. Do you understand that, Alice?"

Alice nodded. She felt a pang of sadness at the thought of losing her friend, but she didn't want to think about that now.

Before she could say anything, the bedroom door flew open and Ben ran in. He leaped onto the bed and started making a noisy fuss about Flame. "I want

Flame to sleep on my bed tonight," he exclaimed.

"Maybe we should see what Flame wants to do," Alice said.

"He wants to sleep with me, don't you, Flame?" Ben said. Grabbing the tiny kitten, he rolled him onto his back and began roughly tickling his white tummy.

Flame squirmed and yowled in protest.

"Careful! You're hurting him!" Alice snapped, grabbing her brother's arm. "Flame's tiny. You have to be very gentle with him."

Ben's face darkened and he thrust Flame at Alice. "You never let me do anything with him!" he said, stamping out of her room.

"Are you okay?" Alice asked Flame worriedly.

Flame nodded, shaking out his ruffled
fur. "I am fine. Ben just surprised me. I do
not think that he meant to hurt me."

Alice bit her lip. Flame was right.
Perhaps she was being overprotective.
Ben was excited about Flame, too, in his
own way.

"Make sure you hide well while I'm
at school, okay?" she said to Flame a few
minutes later.

He looked up at her with bright intelligent eyes. "I will come to school with you, Alice."

"Really? But—" Alice stopped midsentence as she remembered that only she could see Flame when he used his magic to make himself invisible. She grinned. It would be fun having her secret friend with her all day. "All right then. Why not?"

Chapter
FOUR

As Alice was finishing putting on
her uniform, she remembered about the
swimming lesson. Her tummy lurched,
and she felt nervous just thinking about it.

"Is something wrong?" Flame mewed.

Alice explained that she had been
teased by some girls at her old school
who had been jealous about her being
so good at swimming. "I used to like

going swimming before that. Now I'd just rather not bother. Maybe I could leave my bathing suit here and pretend I forgot it."

Flame blinked at her. "Will that mean that you would not have to go into the pool?"

"Probably not. Ms. Ritson will just make me wear one of the school's spare suits, and they're really awful. Anyway, she's on a mission to get us all ready for the meet now. I don't see how I can get out of it." She sighed deeply as she stuffed her swimming things into her schoolbag.

"Maybe your mom can help," Flame suggested.

"I don't want her to know that I still feel like this. She'll get all worried," Alice said.

She hurried downstairs with Flame at her heels. "You'd better stay invisible for now, in case Mom sees you," she whispered to him.

Flame nodded.

Ben was sitting at the table eating a bowl of his favorite cereal. As Alice sat down, her mom put a plate of toast on the table. Alice didn't feel like eating much, so she nibbled a tiny corner of toast.

"Are you feeling all right, honey? You look a bit pale," her mom commented.

"I'm okay," Alice fibbed.

Mrs. Forester frowned. "You're sure nothing's worrying you?"

"Um . . ." The doorbell rang before Alice could reply.

Ben dashed to the door. "I'll get it!"

"That'll be Esme and Luke," Mrs. Forester said, distracted now that the twins had arrived. She went to speak to their mom.

"Phew! That was lucky," Alice said to

Flame. "I thought Mom was going to ask me lots of questions."

Ben bounded back to the kitchen table. "Where's Flame?" he said loudly. "I want to give him some milk before school."

"Give whom some milk?" Mrs. Forester asked as she brought Esme and Luke through to the kitchen.

"That kitt— Ow! What did you do that for?" Ben complained as Alice gave him a kick from under the table.

"Come on, Ben. We'll be late for school," she said, giving him a fierce look.

"But you've got a lot of time before school starts," her mom said, looking puzzled.

"I know. I just want to get there early today . . . ," Alice mumbled vaguely as she grabbed Ben's arm and hustled him into the hall. "You brat!" she scolded, when they were alone. "You nearly gave away our secret!"

Ben's face fell. "I didn't mean to."

"I know you didn't," Alice said, more calmly. "And I didn't mean to blow up at you. Luckily, Mom didn't really hear you. But we'd better go before she starts asking awkward questions."

"Okay," Ben said, shouldering his book bag. "Where *is* Flame, anyway? I've been looking everywhere for him."

"Oh, he's probably under my bed asleep," Alice fibbed. There was no way she could tell Ben that Flame was sitting on the doormat, right behind him—invisible to everyone except her!

"There are lots of kids around, and it can be slippery around the pool," Alice said to Flame worriedly, as she was getting changed. "You could get stepped on or something."

The girls' locker room had new white tiles and smelled of fresh paint. The sound of her classmates' voices echoed near Alice's changing room.

Flame was sitting on Alice's folded

school uniform. "I will be very careful to stay out of the way. It will be interesting to watch humans swim."

Alice nodded.

Flame's furry brow wrinkled in a frown as Alice pulled on her bathing suit and then tucked her hair inside her nylon swimming cap. "Why do humans need to put on a second skin to get into the water?" he asked.

"A second . . . ? Oh, you mean my bathing suit. Well, I can't go swimming with nothing on! I'm not wearing a fur coat like you are!" Alice said, grinning. "And we have to wear swimming caps. It's the rules. But to tell the truth they're a bit useless for keeping your hair dry."

As Alice headed for the foot bath

at the entrance to the pool, Flame went off in the opposite direction.

Ms. Ritson was standing poolside, bending down to give instructions to the swimmers already in the water. She wore a white T-shirt and track pants and had a whistle around her neck. Her straight brown hair was tied into two bunches.

Some other teachers were with their own classes in different parts of the pool.

Alice walked quickly over to the steps leading down into the shallow end, hoping to get into the water before Ms. Ritson saw her and made a fuss. But there was a line of kids already waiting at the steps, and Alice had to wait her turn.

Ms. Ritson straightened up. She

looked around and saw Alice. "Ah,
Alice," she said, coming over. "I haven't
forgotten our conversation in class.
Now don't worry if you're a bit nervous
about swimming. We'll take it very
slowly, all right?"

"Yes, ma'am," Alice mumbled, going
bright red.

She knew Ms. Ritson was just trying
to be nice. But it didn't make the horrible
feeling in her tummy any better.

Alice got into the pool, trying not
to look at the others splashing around
without a care. She remembered when
swimming had been lots of fun for her,
too, before the girls at her old school
started teasing her.

She moved along to stand with three
other girls who were nervously gripping

the side of the pool and shivering.

Ms. Ritson was blowing up orange water wings. She threw them to Alice's three classmates.

"I don't need water wings, ma'am," Alice said quickly.

Ms. Ritson pointed to a pile of square white floats. "You can use one of these, instead."

"Okay!" Alice quickly reached up and grabbed a float. Holding the float out in front with extended arms, she pushed gingerly off the side and kicked out with her legs.

"Very good, Alice. That's the way," Ms. Ritson called out encouragingly.

Alice swam slowly back and forth, doing laps with the float. She made sure not to go so quickly that Ms. Ritson could figure out that she was a good swimmer. None of the other girls noticed Alice, which was fine by her.

Letting herself drift, Alice glanced over toward the pool's snack bar. Flame's tiny figure was curled up on one of the seats.

After quickly checking that no one was watching, Alice waved at him.

She saw Flame lift his head and prick his ears, before jumping off the chair. He leaped down the balcony steps and came trotting purposefully down the side of the pool.

He must have thought I was waving to him because I'm in trouble, Alice thought. *I'd better go and tell him that I'm fine.*

Bracing her hands on the edge of the pool, she jumped up and heaved herself out onto the side. As she was straightening up, a group of boys came out of the locker room and surrounded Flame's invisible body. Tim Wagnall was one of them.

Alice tensed as she saw Flame trying to navigate his way around the boys' legs.

Tim elbowed one of the others in the ribs. "Last one in the pool's a rotten egg!" he cried.

"You're on!"

Tim and the other boy started running.

One of the teachers blew her whistle and put up her hands. "Slow down, you two!"

Tim waved to show he'd heard her, but as soon as the teacher turned back around, he grinned mischievously and aimed a play-kick at the boy beside him.

Flame had been just about to run past when Tim's bare foot hit him and lifted him off his feet. He yowled with terror as he shot through the air and hurtled toward the pool!

Chapter
FIVE

Flame landed in the water with a tiny splash!

As he surfaced, Alice could see his tiny legs thrashing as he tried to stay afloat.

"Hey! Where did that kitten come from?" Tim cried.

Alice gasped. The shock must have made Flame forget to stay invisible.

Now he couldn't use his magic without giving himself away!

Without a second thought, Alice sprang off the side and dived in.

She kicked out strongly in a front crawl, cutting cleanly through the water. Her classmates lined up by the side of the pool, but she didn't notice.

She reached Flame's tiny soaked figure as he started to sink. Alice reached out, grabbed the scruff of his neck, and yanked him to the surface. Flame whimpered in terror, coughing up water.

"I've got you now!" she said, drawing him close and treading water.

Flame seemed to be in a blind panic. He scrabbled at her arms, instinctively trying to find a safe foothold.

"Oh!" Alice gasped as his sharp claws
raked her skin. She quickly flipped onto
her back and settled him on her chest.
"Flame! Calm down," she whispered.

Shivering and trembling, but calmer
now, Flame lay on Alice's chest as she
did a backstroke over to the steps.

As one of the teachers helped Alice
climb out, a cheer went up. All the kids
were crowding around and clapping.

"She saved that kitten!" someone cried.

"Did you see that amazing dive?" said another kid.

"Way to go, Alice!" shouted Tim Wagnall.

Alice's cheeks burned. She wished they'd all stop making such a fuss. She was sure the teasing was about to start at any moment. Keeping her head down and holding Flame close, she pushed through them all.

"Not so fast, Alice! I want a word with you." Ms. Ritson stepped out to bar her way.

Alice nimbly wove around her and hurried toward the locker room. "In a minute, ma'am," she shouted over her shoulder.

Once she was inside, Alice threw herself into a changing stall and bolted the door. Grabbing her towel, she wrapped the shivering kitten in it and began gently patting him dry.

Flame began purring faintly. "Thank you, Alice. You were very brave to dive in and rescue me. I know how you scared you must have been."

"I didn't really have time to think about it," Alice realized. "I just knew I couldn't bear it if anything happened to you."

Now that all the excitement was over, her scratched arms began stinging. Alice winced at their soreness.

Flame's bright green eyes narrowed with concern. "But I have hurt you. Let me make you better."

Bright silver sparks appeared in
Flame's damp fur inside the towel, and
there was a faint crackling sound. The
tiny kitten leaned toward Alice and huffed
out a glittery mist. Alice felt Flame's

warm breath settle on her scratches.
The tingling increased for a second
and then suddenly all the pain melted
away and all sign of the scratches
faded.

"Come out of there at once,
Alice!" Ms. Ritson ordered, sounding
upset and banging on the changing
stall door. "And bring that kitten
with you! Though goodness only
knows how it got into here in the
first place!"

"Uh-oh," Alice whispered to Flame.
"Now I'm in trouble. You'd better make
sure you stay invisible now."

Flame nodded.

"I'm coming, ma'am," Alice called,
buying herself some time.

Shivering, she draped her towel

around her head and shoulders. Alice
took a deep breath and unbolted the
changing stall door.

Ms. Ritson stood there with her
hands on her hips. "Are you ready to
tell me what's going on now, Alice? And
where's that kitten?"

"I don't know. It . . . um, ran off.
It must be a stray or something," Alice
said, with her head bowed.

Ms. Ritson peered into the
changing stall suspiciously, but she
couldn't see Flame, who was curled
up invisibly on Alice's school uniform.
"I'll get someone to look around for it
later. But what I'd really like to know,
young lady, is how you changed from
a nervous beginner into an excellent
swimmer in about sixty seconds."

Alice gulped, racking her brains for something to say.

"I'm waiting," Ms. Ritson said.

"I . . . It must be a miracle," Alice burst out. "Yes, that's it! My thin blood has just got better all by itself. I bet it was the shock of diving in. As soon as I was in deep water, my arms and legs just started moving by themselves and suddenly—I could swim. Isn't it amazing? I'm definitely not sure it could ever happen again . . . ," she babbled.

"Alice," Ms. Ritson said warningly, "I've had just about enough of this."

Alice's shoulders slumped. She realized that it was time to tell her teacher the truth. "I've . . . um, always been a good swimmer," she admitted.

"Then why did you pretend you could hardly swim at all?"

"I didn't exactly say that. I just let you *think* I meant that," Alice went on miserably. "The thing is . . . I was the best swimmer in my class at my old school. And some of the girls thought I was showing off. They teased me about it all the time, so I started trying to get out of swimming lessons."

Ms. Ritson frowned. "I understand now. That must have been really awful for you," she said gently. "But not everyone gets jealous when they see others doing well. I'm certain that no one here is going to tease you. Your classmates were really impressed by the way you dived in and saved that kitten."

"Were they?" Alice asked uncertainly, still having trouble believing this.

"I can see that you're not convinced. I'll prove it to you," Ms. Ritson said. "Come with me."

Trying not to drag her feet, Alice nervously followed the teacher to the changing stall door. Ms. Ritson opened the door a crack, so that she and Alice could hear the other kids talking outside in the pool area.

"Did you see Alice's amazing dive?"

"Yeah! It was really cool."

"She's a fantastic swimmer. I hope she's on my team for the meet."

Alice's eyes widened as she heard all the good comments. She finally realized that Ms. Ritson was right. Her new classmates weren't jealous of her at all! She breathed a long-overdue sigh of relief as she realized that she was going to be able

to relax and enjoy her swimming lessons from now on.

Alice turned to the teacher. "Thanks, ma'am!" she said, her eyes shining.

"You're welcome. Just one more thing, before you get showered and changed," Ms. Ritson said seriously.

"Yes?"

"If you have any problems from now on, speak to me or your mom about it. Promise?"

Alice blushed, but she felt a grin stretching from ear to ear. "Promise!" she agreed.

Chapter
SIX

"Everyone's talking about how you dived into the pool to save a gray-and-white kitten. It was Flame, wasn't it?" Ben said, as he and Alice walked home after the bell had rung.

"Um . . . yeah. He must have jumped into my school bag when I wasn't looking," Alice said hastily. "But . . . I . . . um, ran home at lunchtime and took him back up to my bedroom."

Ben dragged his bookbag on the floor behind him. "I never get to spend time with Flame," he complained.

Alice realized this was true. All she seemed to do lately, where Flame was concerned, was tell Ben to buzz off.

"How would you like him to sleep on your bed tonight?" *I'm sure Flame won't mind*, she thought.

"Cool! And can I feed him, too?" Ben asked, beaming.

Alice smiled. "Of course you can!"

Over the next few days, Ben was really careful to be gentle with Flame. He helped Alice smuggle food up to her bedroom for him and was delighted when Flame slept on his bed for a second night.

"I washed Flame's food bowl," Ben said to Alice, one evening just before bedtime. "We have to be careful Mom doesn't see it."

Alice smiled. Ben hadn't sulked for ages, and he was being really protective of Flame now. "Thanks, Ben. See you in the morning," she said.

"Night, Alice."

The following morning, Flame lay stretched out on Alice's comforter, looking relaxed and content as she was getting ready for school.

"I'm getting along well with everyone in swim class now," Alice said. "I don't have to worry being teased at all, and I can just concentrate on improving my stroke."

Flame nodded. "You are a very good swimmer, Alice."

"Thanks! I'm not bad," she said modestly.

The extra practice at the after-school club was helping, too. Alice's mom was happy for her to go along for an hour on two evenings a week.

Today was Monday, and Alice felt excited and a tiny bit nervous. Ms. Ritson was going to be picking the teams for the swim meet before the day's normal lesson started.

She finished putting on her school shoes. "Come on, Flame. Let's go and get some breakfast! I want to get to school early to make sure I get picked for lots of teams."

Flame gave an extra-loud purr and trotted after Alice. Out on the landing, she bumped into her mom going into the bathroom. Mrs. Forester was still in her dressing gown. She looked pale and tired.

"Are you okay, Mom?" Alice asked worriedly.

Her mom shook her head carefully. "I woke up with a splitting headache. I'm going to have to take an aspirin."

"Poor you," Alice sympathized. "Why don't you go back to bed and I'll bring you up a cup of tea? Don't worry about

us. I'll get Ben's breakfast and get him
ready for school."

"Thanks, honey, you're a star," her
mom said, smiling weakly. "Just give
me half an hour. I'll be fine by the
time Esme and Luke arrive. Oh, I just
remembered. Ben's school shirt needs
ironing."

"No problem!" Alice said, going
downstairs into the kitchen.

After taking the tea up to her
mom, she got out the ironing board.
As Alice was sorting a shirt out of
the pile of ironing, Ben came into
the kitchen.

"Where's Mom?" he asked.

Alice explained about the headache.

"Oh. Can I have eggs and toast for
breakfast?" Ben asked.

"Sorry. I don't have time to make that. Can you have cereal?"

"If I have to . . ." Ben went to the pantry and took out a box of Chocco Blasts. He shook the box. "This is almost empty. And I don't like anything else." He stamped over to the table and sat there with his chin in his hands. "I guess I'll just have to starve," he moaned.

Alice sighed. She didn't need this right now.

She felt a tiny paw pat her ankle and looked down to see Flame beckoning to her to follow him. The moment he scampered into the laundry room, there was a tiny flash and a fountain of sparks.

A plastic shopping bag appeared

out of thin air. Inside it was a mega-size box of Chocco Blasts.

"Wow! Thanks, Flame. But could you make the box a bit small—" she began, and then she stopped hurriedly as Ben came in.

He immediately spotted the enormous box of cereal. "Hey! Great! Mom must

have got these on sale!" Wrapping both arms around the box, he went into the kitchen with it.

"Let me help you pour some out," Alice said, following him.

"I want to do it!" Ben exclaimed.

He tore open the box and aimed it awkwardly at the empty bowl. A landslide of Chocco Blasts shot out.

They overflowed the bowl, piled up on the kitchen table, and shot all over the floor with a spattering noise.

"Oh, great! Now I'll have to vacuum all this up!" Alice grumbled.

Ben wasn't listening. "This is awesome!" he said, sloshing milk around and shoveling chocolate cereal into his mouth.

"I am sorry, Alice. I was trying to help," Flame mewed softly.

"I know you were. Never mind. At least Ben's happy!" she whispered, going back to ironing his shirt.

Ten minutes and three bowls of cereal later, Ben got down from the table. He had a sticky rim of chocolate-colored drool around his mouth. "Don't feel very well," he murmured.

"I'm not surprised. You've really been pigging out!" Alice said, wiping his mouth with a paper towel. "Put this shirt on and don't you dare be sick!"

As Ben finished dressing and then went off to change for school, Alice heard her mom moving around upstairs. "Oh no! Mom's getting up. She must be feeling better. I'll never have time to clean this up!"

"Do not worry," Flame purred. He pointed a tiny front paw and there was another crackle as a fountain of sparks shot toward the table. The box of Chocco Blasts shrank to normal size, and all the spilled cereal and pools of milk melted away with a fizzing sound.

"Phew! Thanks, Flame. Quick, can you jump into my bookbag? Let's grab Ben and head off to school before he says anything to Mom!"

Chapter
SEVEN

". . . and finally, Tim Wagnall and
Alice Forester. That makes up the
relay team," Ms. Ritson said, finishing
choosing teams for all the races.

"Yay!" Alice cried, jumping up
and down. She was also in the girls'
breaststroke, the mixed front crawl,
and the interclass race, but her all-time
favorite was the relay race.

She glanced over to where Flame
was curled up on a windowsill. Quickly
checking that no one was looking, she
gave him a sneaky thumbs-up.

"The pool's grand opening is next
Saturday, so it'll be closed on Friday to
get ready for the celebrations. We have
a special guest coming to do the honors:
Judy Blasket."

"She's an actress from *Ivygreen*—my mom's favorite TV soap opera! Just wait until I tell her," Alice said excitedly.

"We're hoping Judy will attract a big crowd!" Ms. Ritson smiled. "Okay everyone, you have four days to practice your swimming, including today's lesson. So grab your stuff and we'll go straight across to the pool."

"Great! Come on, team. Let's grab a relay baton and start practicing!" Tim jumped up and did one of his front-crawl impressions across the room and out into the hallway.

The other kids laughed, but Alice couldn't bring herself to join in. She still hadn't quite forgiven Tim for kicking Flame into the pool. She knew it had been an accident, but it wouldn't have

happened if Tim wasn't always fooling
around.

"Can you stay over by the snack bar
this time? I don't want anything else to
happen to you," she whispered to Flame.

Flame nodded and gave her a furry
grin. "I do not feel like going into the
pool again!"

As Ms. Ritson blew her whistle for
the end of the lesson, Alice climbed out
of the pool.

Her muscles ached, but she didn't
feel a bit tired. She'd swum really well
today. In relay practice, she'd passed the
baton smoothly at each change-over. She
couldn't wait for the meet on Saturday.

"Well done, Alice. I'm glad to see
you enjoying yourself," Ms. Ritson

commented. "I think I picked the right girl for our relay team."

Alice beamed at her. "I hope so, ma'am!"

Some of the kids were grabbing their towels from the radiators, where they'd left them earlier, and going up to get hot drinks from the snack bar.

Alice wrapped herself in her warm towel and also headed for the snack bar.

She was looking forward to telling Flame how great swimming had been today.

But when she reached the snack bar, she couldn't see him anywhere. She checked beneath all the chairs and tables, but there was no sign of him.

Maybe he was waiting for her in the locker room. Alice went straight back to her changing stall. But Flame wasn't there, either.

After showering and dressing in double-quick time, Alice hurried back to the classroom and arrived before everybody else. She looked for Flame on the windowsill and the tops of the cabinets.

But there was still no sign of him.

After checking under all the desks,
Alice sank into her seat. She wasn't sure
what to do next. "Flame? Where are you?"
she said out loud, worried.

There was a very faint whimper. It
sounded as if it had come from inside her
bookbag.

"Flame?" Picking up her bag, Alice
slipped her hand inside. "Ah, there you
are . . ." Her fingers brushed against a
tightly curled furry little bundle.

She was so glad to have found him
that it took her a moment to realize that
the tiny kitten was trembling all over.
Alice felt a stir of alarm as she opened the
bag up wider. A pair of troubled emerald
eyes glowed at her from the interior.

"What's wrong? Are you sick?" she
asked gently.

"My uncle's spies are very close,"
Flame whined in terror.

Alice bit back a gasp. The moment
she had been dreading was here. Flame
was in terrible danger. Even though she
hated to think of losing her friend, she
knew she was going to have to be strong.

"Are . . . are you leaving now?" she
asked.

Flame shook his head. "I will hide

in here. My enemies may pass me by, and
then I will be able to stay with you."

"Right! We're leaving! I'll find
somewhere else to hide you. I just have
to think of something to tell Ms. Ritson."
Alice decided.

"No, Alice. That would just draw
attention to me," he interrupted. "Just
leave me here for a little while." Flattening
his ears, Flame curled into an even
tighter ball.

"All right," Alice whispered.

As her classmates began filing into the room, Alice tucked the bag with the terrified kitten inside under her desk.

Alice's chest felt tight as she tried to push away the awful thought that Flame could still be found at any moment. She didn't know how she was going to concentrate on her work, but there was nothing else she could do.

Chapter
EIGHT

Alice hardly dared look inside her bookbag. Somehow she resisted checking on Flame until it was time to go home.

Her heart was beating fast as she opened her bag.

Flame was gone.

"Oh!" Alice gasped, biting back tears. She felt a wave of sadness wash over her. She hadn't even said good-bye.

Alice went to meet Ben. As they
walked home together, she felt as if she
was in a daze.

"Are you okay?" Ben asked worriedly.

Alice nodded. "I'm just tired, that's all."
She didn't feel up to telling him about
Flame yet.

Back home, she dumped her coat and bag in the hall and went straight upstairs. Ben was just coming out of her bedroom.

"What are you doing in my room?" she snapped, before she could stop herself.

Ben blinked at her in surprise. "I was just saying hello to Flame. I'm going downstairs to watch TV now."

"I'm sorry, Ben. I didn't mean to shout at—" Alice stopped and did a double take. "Did you say—Flame?"

"Yeah," Ben said, giving her a funny look.

Alice shot into her room. Flame was sitting on her bed washing his gray-and-white fur. He looked up as she came in, and she saw that the tip of his tiny pink tongue was still hanging out.

"Oh, Flame. You came back!" she exclaimed, giving him a cuddle.

An enormous happy grin spread over Alice's face. She thought she might burst with happiness.

"I laid a false trail and escaped my uncle's spies," Flame purred. "But if they come again, I may have to leave at once."

"I'm just glad you're here now!" Alice said.

Flame's bright emerald eyes crinkled in a smile. "So am I. I am looking forward to watching you swim in the meet!"

Alice felt excited as she and Flame, her mom, and Ben walked through the school gates on Saturday and joined the crowds already there.

Strips of colored paper and bunches of balloons hung outside the pool building. A huge banner read MELDWAY SCHOOL SWIMMING POOL, GRAND OPENING.

Alice saw a fancy car pull up. A pretty blond woman, wearing bright makeup, a jade-green dress, and lots of jewelry, got out.

"That's the actress from Mom's favorite soap opera," she whispered to Flame.

Flame was in her bookbag. He had his head sticking out and was watching everything with great interest.

Everyone cheered as Judy Blasket smiled and waved. The principal gave a speech and then the glamorous actress cut the ribbon and declared the new pool open.

As a man from the local paper began taking photos, Alice and Flame and all the other children taking part in the meet went inside to get changed.

"See you in there!" Alice called to her mom and Ben.

"All right, honey!" Mrs. Forester called from the line of people waiting to get Judy Blasket's autograph.

In the locker room, excited voices filled the air. Alice's whole class was taking part in the meet, so she had to share a changing stall with a classmate.

"Where are you going to be today?" she whispered to Flame worriedly, once the other girl had gone out.

"I found a safe ledge to sit on
when I was laying a false trail for my
enemies," Flame mewed.

"Okay. I'll see you after the meet.
Wish me luck!" Alice picked Flame up.
Breathing in his sweet kitten smell, she
kissed the top of his head.

"Good luck, Alice," Flame said
with an extra-big purr.

As Alice emerged from the foot
bath, she saw that the pool looked even
bigger and more impressive with seats
lining the sides and so many people
watching. The snack-bar area was full of
spectators, too.

Alice's tummy did a flip with nerves
and excitement. But it was a good
feeling. She never would have dreamed
that she'd be swimming in front of
all these people *and* have her new
classmates cheering her on.

The races began, and the sound of
cheers and splashing echoed around the
building. Then it was time for Alice's
first race, the girls' breaststroke.

She had butterflies in her tummy
as she lined up with the other
competitors.

"On your marks! Get set . . ."

Ph-eeep! As the whistle blew, Alice flung herself into a dive. She surfaced and started swimming. Her nerves settled down instantly, and all she could think about was swimming to the finish as fast as possible.

A cheer went up as the race ended. Alice had come in third. She was third in the mixed front crawl and came in second with the rest of her class in the interclass race.

In between watching the other races, Alice glanced to the back of the pool where she could see Flame's tiny figure sitting below one of the tall windows.

Flame saw her looking. He waved a tiny front paw and a cloud of bright pink sparks shot out. They floated

upward and briefly formed the shape of
a glittering pink butterfly.

Alice smiled as the butterfly fluttered
over toward her. She held up her hand
and the butterfly settled for a moment,
before dissolving into glittering, invisible
dust.

"Thanks, Flame," Alice breathed.
It was good to know that he was
supporting her in his own special way.

The relay race was the final race of
the day.

Alice stood ready with her other
team members. One of the boys went
first, followed by a girl. Alice watched
tensely. Her team was starting to fall
behind. There were about three feet to
make up already.

Then it was Tim's turn. As their team

member swam to the side, Tim got ready
to take the baton. He leaned out and
went to grasp it.

"Oh," Alice gasped. Tim had
dropped the baton!

"Quick, jump in and get it!" she
urged.

Tim jumped in. He splashed
around and finally grabbed the floating
baton. Pushing off the side, he started
swimming.

Alice's spirits sank as Tim swam
to the deep end and then turned to
swim back. He tried his best, but by
the time he raised the baton for Alice
to take it, he was half a length behind
everyone else.

Alice was never going to be able
to make up the distance.

Alice leaned out and grasped the baton. *Yes!* She had it. Holding it tight, she hurled herself into a shallow dive. As she surfaced, she was already stretching out in a powerful front crawl.

Kicking her legs and concentrating on her over-arm stroke, she powered toward the deep end. Gritting her teeth, Alice swam as if her life depended on it. At the turn, she was barely two feet behind the leader.

As she swam back toward the finish, Alice gradually drew level with the lead swimmer.

"Come on, Alice!" yelled Tim.

"You can do it!" shouted Ms. Ritson.

Nine feet to the finish! Alice and the lead swimmer were neck-and-neck. Alice used every last bit of her strength in a final spurt. She stretched out and her fingers touched the edge a microsecond before the other girl.

She'd won the race for her team!

"Yes!" Alice threw her arms in the air.

Cheers and clapping broke out as Alice climbed out of the pool. She couldn't stop smiling.

"Well done!" Mrs. Forester shouted. Alice looked over to see her mom and

Ben hugging each other and jumping up and down. She waved at them.

Alice's team members congratulated her. Tim Wagnall looked like he was about to throw his arms around her neck.

"Whoa!" Alice took a step back. That was going *too* far!

Tim got the message. "That was *so* amazing. You're a great swimmer—for a girl!" he joked.

Alice shook her head. Tim would never change. But she would still rather be in this class in her new school than anywhere else!

Alice was glad that Flame was safe up on the windowsill. There was no way that she could sneak over to see him with all the fuss still going on.

After the applause died down, there
was a break before the awards ceremony.
Alice slipped away to wash her hair.
Most people had stayed where they
were and the girls' locker room was
empty.

As Alice took off her cap and
went to fetch her shampoo from her
changing stall, there was a blinding
white flash.

"Oh!" she gasped, rubbing her eyes.

Flame stood there, looking
magnificent as his true lion self. Silver
sparkles glittered in his thick white fur.
This time, next to Flame, there stood an
older gray lion with a wise expression.

And then Alice knew that her
friend was really leaving this time. "Your
enemies have come back, haven't they?"

she asked, her voice breaking.

"Yes, they have. And now I must go,"
Flame's deep gentle voice rumbled.

Alice ran forward and threw her
arms around Flame's muscular neck.
"I'm really going to miss you. I'll never
forget you!" she said tearfully. She forced
herself to stand back. "Go! Quickly! Save
yourself!"

Flame nodded. "You have been a

good friend. Be well, Alice."

The old gray lion smiled at Alice and there was a last bright flash and a burst of sparks that showered down around her and sizzled on the wet tiles. Flame and the gray lion faded and then finally disappeared.

Alice stood there, her heart aching and her throat tight with tears.

"Alice! There you are!" called one of her classmates. "Ms. Ritson sent me to find you. The awards ceremony is about to start."

"I'll be there in a minute!" Alice took a deep breath as she thought about the adventure she had shared with the magic kitten. Flame would be her special secret forever.

As Alice went back toward the

swimming pool, she looked at her team and the awards they were about to receive, and a proud smile pushed away her sadness.

About the Author

Sue Bentley's books for children often include animals or fairies. She lives in Northampton, England, and enjoys reading, going to the movies, and sitting watching the frogs and newts in her garden pond. If she hadn't been a writer, she would probably have been a skydiver or brain surgeon. The main reason she writes is that she can drink pots and pots of tea while she's typing. She has met and owned many cats, and each one has brought a special sort of magic to her life.

Don't miss these Magic Kitten books!

Don't miss these Magic Ponies books!

Don't miss these Magic Puppy books!

Don't miss these Magic Bunny books!